The Garden

written by Suzette Toms
illustrated by Lamia Aziz

Grandpa was happy about his vegetable garden. He did some work there every day. He took out the weeds and put water on the plants. He grew good vegetables all the time.

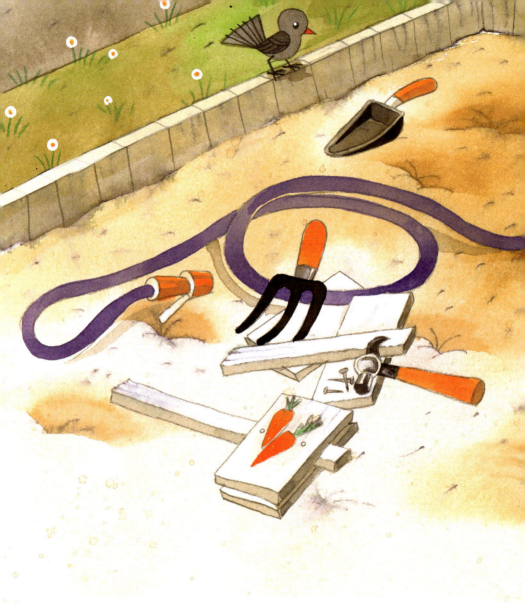

One day he put in some carrot seeds and peas. He gave them water and they grew big.

Soon Grandpa saw that the carrots didn't look right. Then he picked some pea pods and found there were no peas inside! How could this happen? It was a mystery!

Grandpa was very sad. His garden had never been like this before! Something wasn't right!

He didn't know what to do about it.
How could he stop bad things from
happening? His garden didn't look
good anymore.

One day Grandma found out what was happening. She saw their grandson, George, going to the garden. The next day Grandma saw him going that way again. He had a can of water in his hand. She watched him through the kitchen window.

George pulled a carrot out of the garden. He washed it in his can of water. He bit off the carrot and ate it! Then he put the green top back in the garden!

Next, George ate all the peas out of a pea pod. He left the pod with no peas on the plant!

Grandma was cross with George. She took him into the house. She made him tell Grandpa what a bad thing he had done.

Grandpa wanted to laugh. He was happy that the mystery was over. But he wanted George to find out about hard work in a garden.

Grandpa got George to do the work for him. He had to water the garden and look after it every day. After a long time, new carrots and peas were ready.